Sabrina
The Teenage Witch ™

Dream Date

By Margo Lundell
"SABRINA, THE TEENAGE WITCH"
Based on Characters Appearing in Archie Comics

Developed for Television by Jonathan Schmock
Based on the Episode Written by Rachel Lipman

Simon Spotlight

Photographs by Don Cadette

 SIMON SPOTLIGHT
An imprint of Simon & Schuster Children's Publishing Division
1230 Avenue of the Americas
New York, New York 10020
™Archie Comic Publications Inc. © 1997 Viacom Productions Inc.
SIMON SPOTLIGHT and colophon are registered trademarks of Simon & Schuster.
Manufactured in the United States of America
10 9 8 7 6 5 4 3 2 1
Library of Congress Catalog Card Number 97-67745
ISBN: 0-689-81744-4

Sabrina had a big problem. A school dance at Westbridge High was coming up, and Harvey hadn't invited her to go.

"I wish Harvey wanted to be more than friends," Sabrina told her aunts Zelda and Hilda. "What can I do? I would try a love potion, but I can't find one in my magic book."

Like her aunts, Sabrina was a witch.

"There is no love potion," Aunt Zelda explained. "Because love's too precious to tamper with. But we'll find another way."

Sabrina's best friend, Jenny, refused to worry about a date for the dance. She was going by herself.

"Dates are just society's way of keeping numbers even," Jenny declared at school the next day. "I'm going to represent all things that are odd."

"That's exactly how people will see it," Sabrina replied, shaking her head. "I'd rather have a date."

When Sabrina finally asked Harvey if he planned on going to the dance, he told her he wasn't. "School dances aren't my thing," he said.

Just then Libby, the most popular girl in school, walked up and asked Harvey to the dance. Harvey said he would go! Sabrina was upset.

"I panicked!" Harvey told Sabrina later. "I have a really hard time saying *no*."

Sabrina's aunts knew exactly what to do. On the day of the dance, they mixed a batch of their special Man-Dough and created a date for Sabrina. Sabrina was delighted!

"He'll last about four hours," Zelda told Sabrina. "Just long enough for the dance."

Hilda admitted that the Man-Dough date had a flaw—he was too enthusiastic. Hilda had poured more enthusiasm into the personality glaze than she should have.

"Otherwise, your date is tall, dark, and yeasty!" Hilda joked.

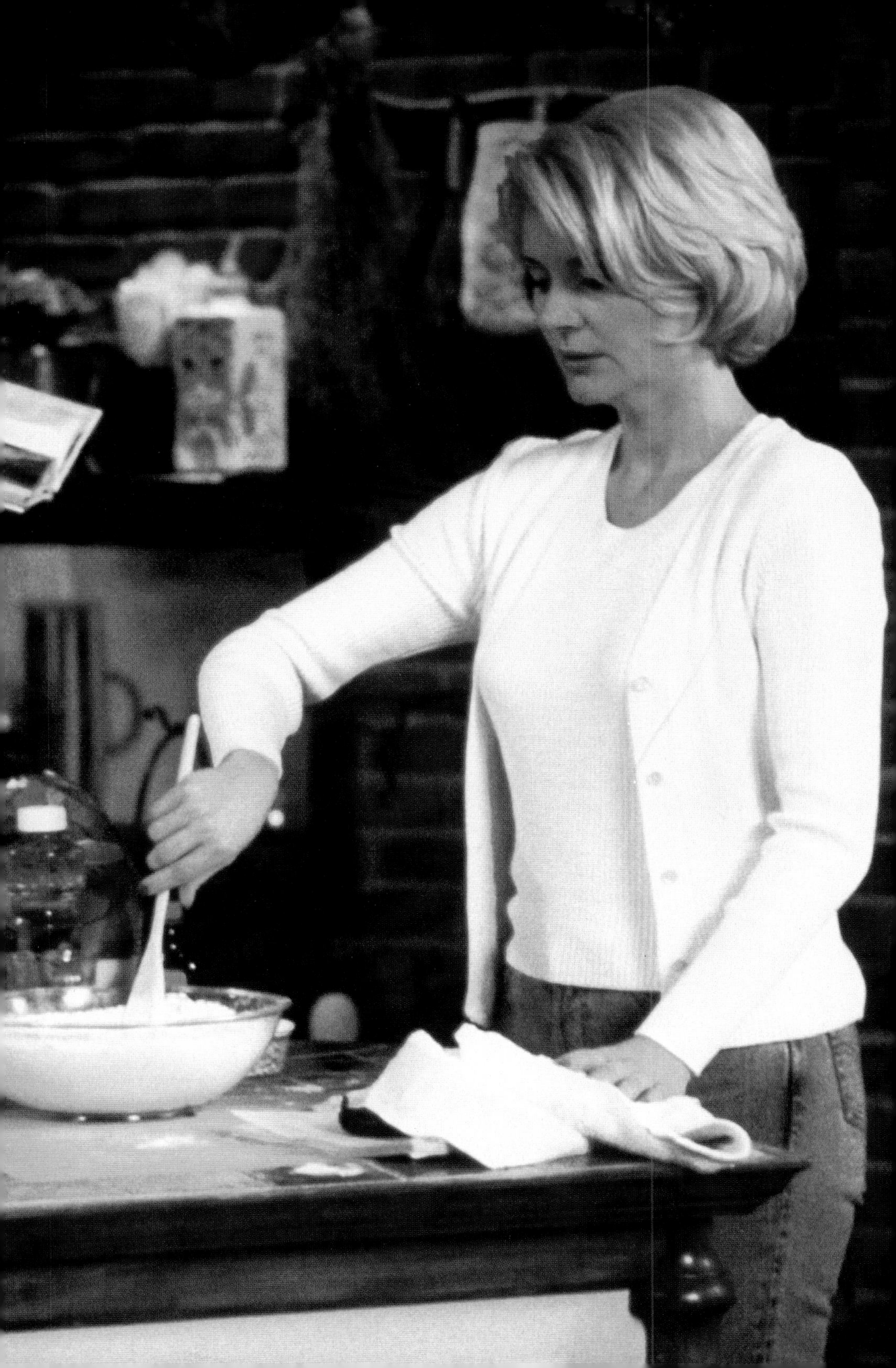

Later that evening, the dance had already started when Sabrina and her dough date got to school. Jenny saw them walk into the cafeteria and she went up to Sabrina.

"Hi," said Jenny.

"Hi there!" said Sabrina's date in a loud voice.

"Jenny, this is . . . Chad," Sabrina announced, quickly making up a name. "Chad Corey Dylan."

"Great name," Jenny responded.

"Thanks," Sabrina said.

Jenny looked at Sabrina. She had no idea why Sabrina had just thanked her.

Sabrina sent Chad off to get some punch.

"Where did you meet this cute guy?" Jenny asked.

"My aunts introduced us," Sabrina answered. It wasn't really a lie. "What do you think?"

"I approve!" Jenny said.

When Chad came back with the punch, Jenny excused herself, saying she was going to dance.

Chad was surprised. "Dance?" he asked Sabrina. "Do you mean we can dance here?"

"Sure," Sabrina answered. "Do you like dancing?"

"I was made to dance!" Chad shouted, pulling Sabrina toward the dance floor. "And, man, I love this song!"

When Libby and Harvey arrived at the dance, Libby's friend Sasha rushed up to them.

"Where have you been?" she asked. "Wait until you see who brought a fabulous date." Sasha looked in the direction of the dance floor. Libby followed her eyes.

"Oh, no!" Libby cried. "Who is Sabrina with? Come on, Harvey, we have to dance."

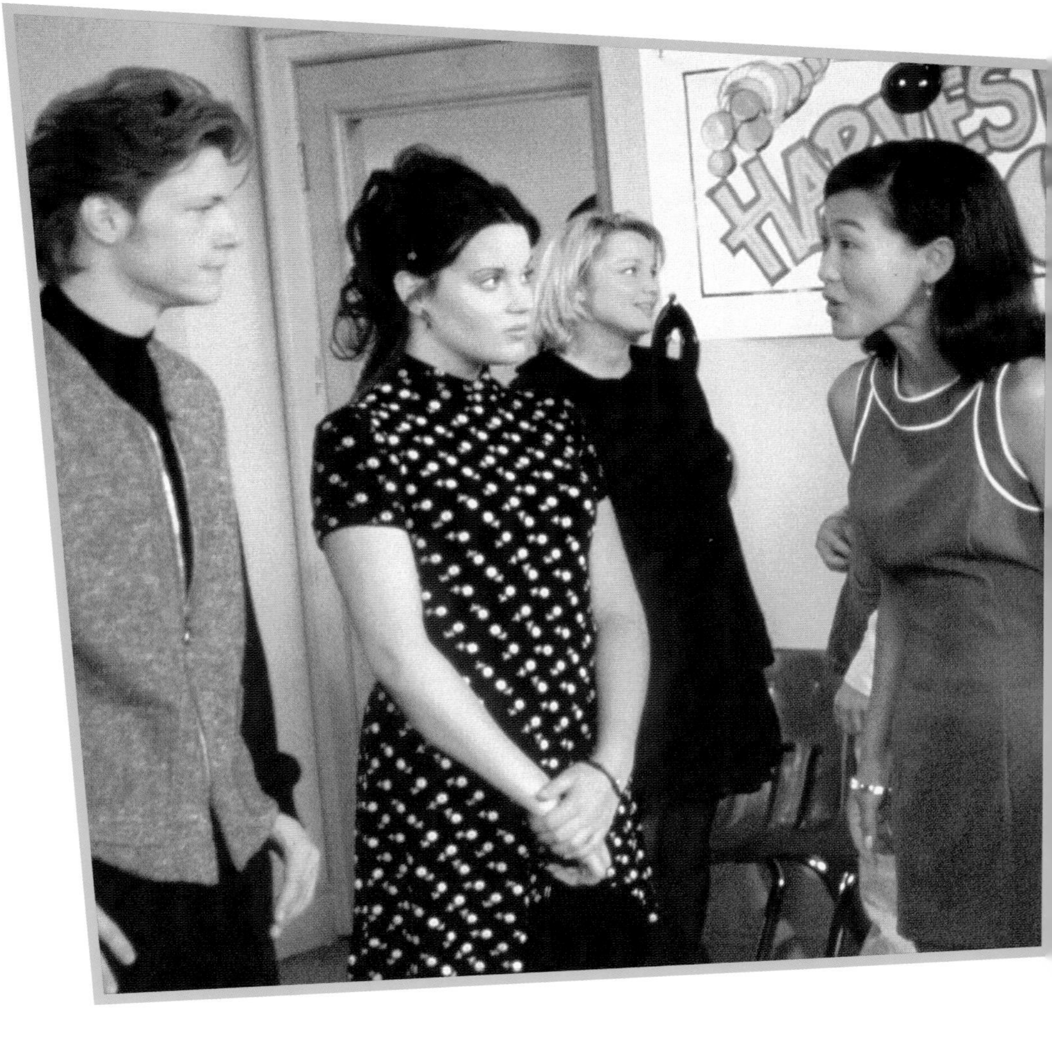

But Harvey refused to dance.

"Actually, I don't dance," he said, looking embarrassed.

"Excuse me?" Libby responded. "This is a dance. Guess what we do here."

Harvey knew Libby was mad at him, but he still wouldn't dance. Libby grabbed Sasha and stomped off to the girls' bathroom.

In the meantime Chad and Sabrina were dancing happily. Chad was an enthusiastic dancer.

"I'm having a great time!" he told Sabrina.

"Me too!" she answered.

Just then Sabrina saw Harvey over by the punch bowl. He was looking at her.

Suddenly Sabrina didn't feel like dancing anymore.

"Look, Chad, I'm sort of tired. Do you mind if I take a breather?" she asked.

"No!" Chad replied. Then he added, "But I have to say, I *love* this song!"

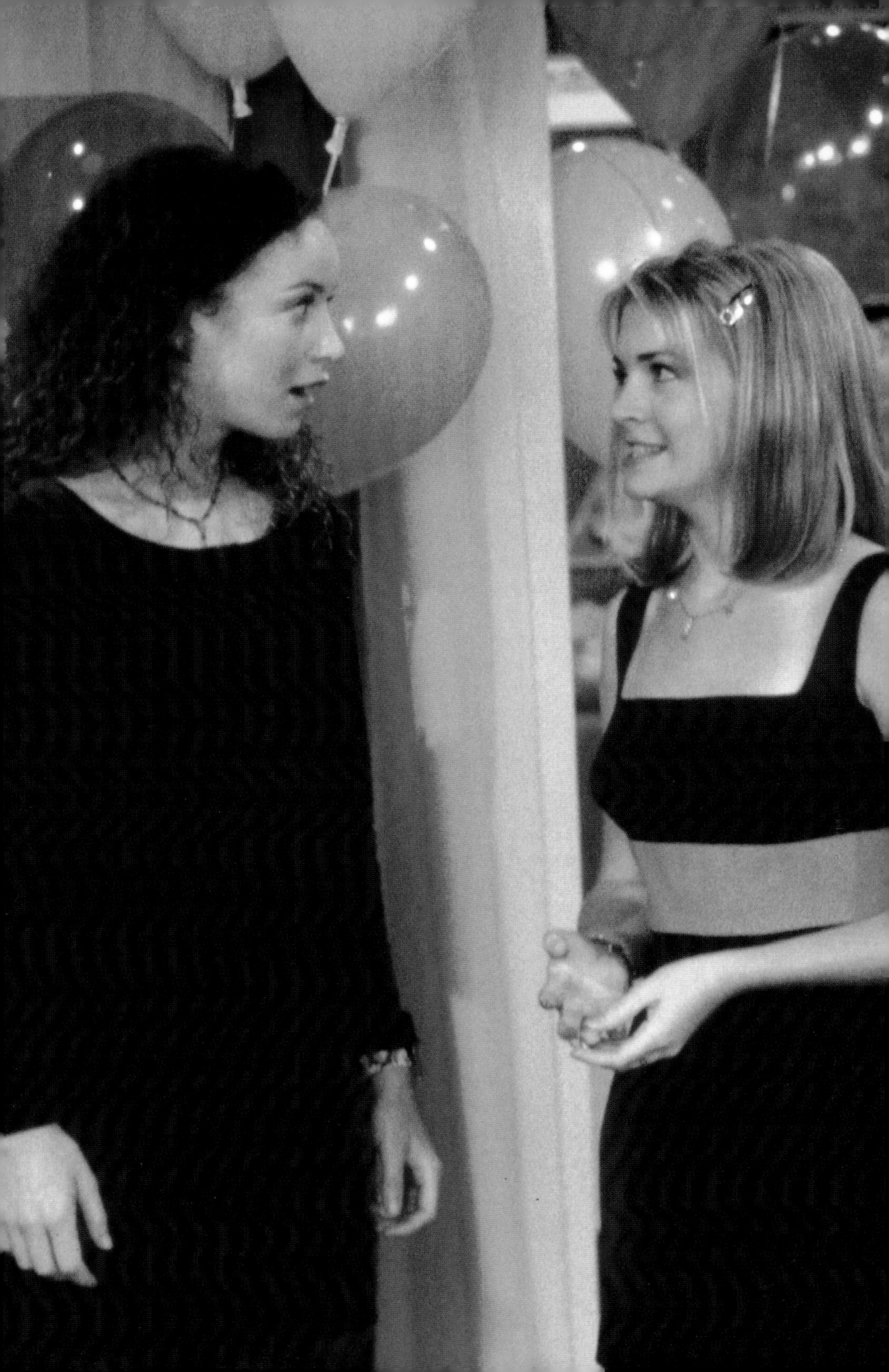

It was clear that Chad wanted to keep dancing. Sabrina found Jenny and asked her to dance with Chad for a while. Then she went over to talk to Harvey.

Harvey was glad to see her and admitted he wasn't having a good time. A few minutes later, Chad came over and introduced himself to Harvey. Then he asked Sabrina to dance with him again, and Sabrina could not say no.

In the meantime Libby and Sasha had come out of the girls' bathroom. They went to sit with Harvey.

"I saw you talking with Chad Corey Dylan," Libby said. "What's he like?"

"Oh, nothing special," Harvey said with a shrug.

Libby sighed. Harvey didn't dance and didn't talk, either. It was going to be a long night.

Chad and Sabrina were dancing again, but Sabrina stopped when a slow dance began.

"Chad, I'm not really into this kind of music," she said. "Let's go stand over by the wall."

"You're a genius!" Chad answered.

When Libby saw Chad and Sabrina walking away from the dance floor, she rushed toward Chad. "Hi, I'm Libby," she said sweetly.

"I'm Chad Corey Dylan," Chad answered.

"Hi, Libby," Sabrina piped up.

"Oh, Sabrina, you're here too!" Libby said, acting surprised to see her. Then she turned back to Chad. "I saw you dancing. You're *good*."

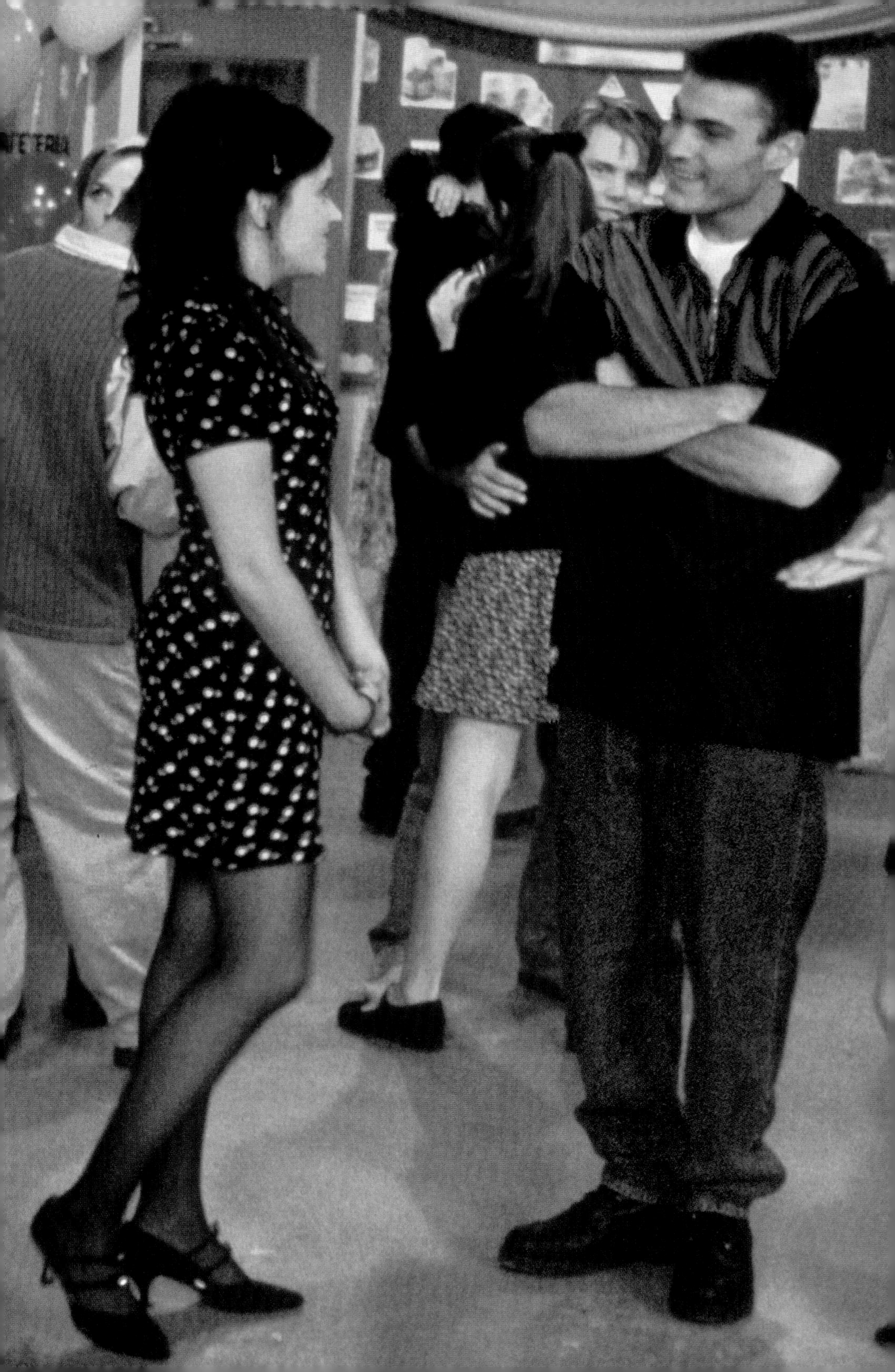

A new song began to play.

"Oh, I love this song!" Chad shouted.

"Me too," Libby agreed. "Unfortunately, my date can't dance."

"Harvey's a *good* dancer!" Sabrina protested. She couldn't stand by and let Harvey look like a loser. Sabrina pointed at his shoes and whispered a magic spell. Then she said, "Harvey, show everybody how well you dance."

Harvey stood up. He seemed to be full of energy.

Harvey began to dance up a storm as everyone watched in amazement.

Sabrina turned to Libby and said, "See? He's actually better than Chad."

"Much better!" Chad agreed.

When the song ended, everybody cheered. Even

Libby was impressed.

"I feel really self-conscious now," Harvey told Libby. "I think I'd better go."

"But I want to dance, Harvey," Libby replied. "You have to dance with me."

"No," Harvey said firmly. "I'm sorry, but I'm going."

When Harvey left the dance, Sabrina ran after him. The two talked outside before deciding to ditch the dance and head for the Slicery to play Foosball.

Harvey waited while Sabrina went back inside to tell Chad.

"Chad, we have to talk," Sabrina said when she found him. "You were sweet to take me to the dance, but you're not the one I want to be with. Harvey's waiting for me outside."

"Excellent choice," Chad said. He sounded only a little hurt. "Harvey's a great guy."

"You really are a dream date," Sabrina answered. "But you can keep dancing. Why don't you ask Libby to dance?"

Chad liked that idea a lot. He looked for Libby while Sabrina went off to meet Harvey.

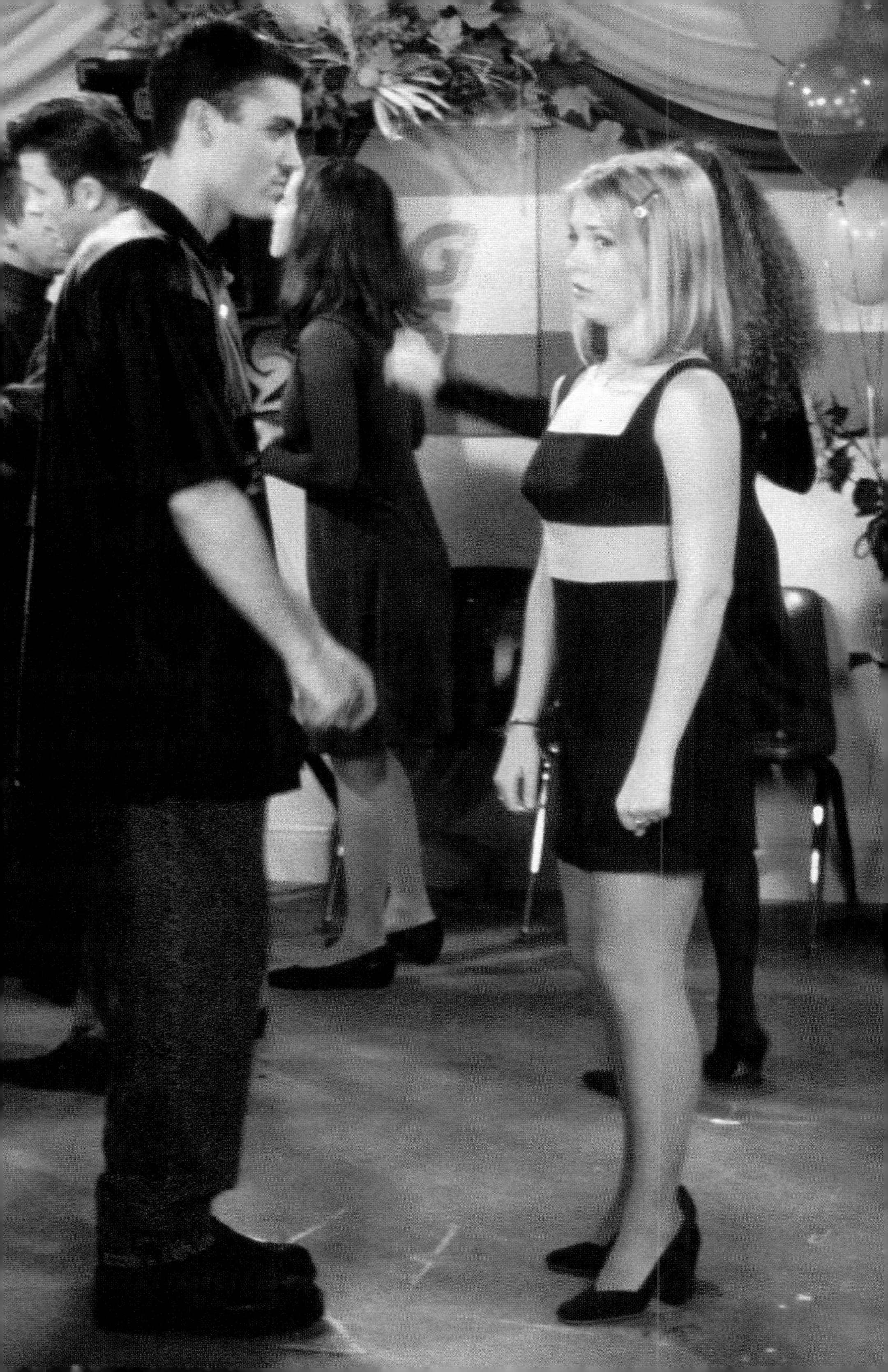

Chad and Libby danced together for a long time. Libby was thrilled. "I'm having the best time, Chad!" she said.

Suddenly Chad coughed, and a powdery spray of flour came out of his mouth. Sabrina's date was turning back into dough!

Chad rushed outside. Libby ran after him, but by the time she got outside, there was nothing but dough on the ground. Libby had no idea she was stepping on chunks of Chad!

It wasn't fair, Libby thought. She had fallen in love with the cutest guy at the dance, and he disappeared!

After playing Foosball with Harvey, Sabrina headed home in a happy haze. When she got there, her aunts asked how her date turned out.

"Great!" Sabrina answered brightly. "But I ended up going to the Slicery with Harvey. I gave my date to Libby."

The two aunts were confused, but Sabrina just kissed them good night and headed off to bed—to dream of Harvey.

SWEEPSTAKES

What would you do with Sabrina's magic powers?

You could win a visit to the set,
a $1000 savings bond, and
other magical prizes!

GRAND PRIZE: A tour of the set of *Sabrina, The Teenage Witch* and a savings bond worth $1000 upon maturity

10 FIRST PRIZES: Sabrina's Cauldron, filled with one Sabrina, The Teenage Witch CD-ROM, one set of eight Archway Paperbacks, one set of three Simon & Schuster children's books, and one Hasbro Sabrina fashion doll

25 SECOND PRIZES: One Sabrina, The Teenage Witch CD-ROM

50 THIRD PRIZES: One Hasbro Sabrina fashion doll

100 FOURTH PRIZES: A one-year subscription to Sabrina, The Teenage Witch comic book, published by Archie Comics

HASBRO   ARCHWAY PAPERBACK   SIMON & SCHUSTER INTERACTIVE   Archie

Sabrina, The Teenage Witch™ Sweepstakes
Official Rules:

1. No Purchase Necessary. Enter by mailing the completed Official Entry Form or by mailing on a 3″ x 5″ card your name, address, and daytime telephone number to Pocket Books/Sabrina, The Teenage Witch Sweepstakes, 13th Floor, 1230 Avenue of the Americas, NY, NY 10020. Entries must be received by 7/1/98. Not responsible for lost, late, damaged, stolen, illegible, mutilated, incomplete, not delivered entries, or for typographical errors in the entry form or rules. Entries are void if they are in whole or in part illegible, incomplete, or damaged. Enter as often as you wish, but each entry must be mailed separately. Winners will be selected at random from all eligible entries received in a drawing to be held on or about 7/7/98. Winners will be notified by mail.

2. Prizes: One Grand Prize: A weekend (four days/three nights) trip to Los Angeles for two people including round-trip coach airfare from the major airport nearest the winner's residence, ground transportation or car rental, meals, three nights in a hotel (one room, occupancy for two), and a tour of the set of Sabrina, The Teenage Witch (approximate retail value $3500.00) and a savings bond worth $1000 (SUS) upon maturity in 18 years. Travel accommodations are subject to availability; certain restrictions apply. 10 First Prizes: Sabrina's Cauldron, filled with one CD-ROM (a Windows 95 compatible program), one set of eight Sabrina, The Teenage Witch books published by Archway Paperbacks, one set of three Simon & Schuster Children's books, and one Hasbro Sabrina fashion doll (approximate retail value $100). 25 Second Prizes: Sabrina, The Teenage Witch CD-ROM, published by Simon & Schuster Interactive (approximate retail value $30). 50 Third Prizes: Sabrina, The Teenage Witch doll (approximate retail value $17.99). 100 Fourth Prizes: a one-year subscription to Sabrina, The Teenage Witch comic book, published by Archie Comics (approximate retail value $15). The Grand Prize must be taken on the dates specified by sponsors.

3. The sweepstakes is open to legal residents of the U.S. and Canada (excluding Quebec). Prizes will be awarded to the winner's parent or legal guardian if under 18. Any minor taking a Grand Prize trip must be accompanied by a parent or legal guardian. Void in Puerto Rico and wherever prohibited or restricted by law. All federal, state, and local laws apply. Employees of Viacom International, Inc., their families living in the same household, and its subsidiaries and their affiliates and their respective agencies and participating retailers are not eligible.

4. One prize per person or household. Prizes are not transferable and may not be substituted except by sponsors, in event of prize unavailability, in which case a prize of equal or greater value will be awarded. All prizes will be awarded. The odds of winning a prize depend upon the number of eligible entries received.

5. If a winner is a Canadian resident, then he/she must correctly answer a skill-based question administered by mail.

6. All expenses on receipt and use of prize, including federal, state, and local taxes, are the sole responsibility of the winners. Winners may be required to execute and return an Affidavit of Eligibility and Release and all other legal documents that the sweepstakes sponsor may require (including a W-9 tax form) within 15 days of attempted notification or an alternate winner will be selected. Grand Prize Winner's travel companion will be required to execute a liability release prior to ticketing.

7. By accepting a prize, winners or winners' parents or legal guardians on winners' behalf agree to allow use of their names, photographs, likenesses, and entries for any advertising, promotion, and publicity purposes without further compensation to or permission from the entrants, except where prohibited by law.

8. By participating in this sweepstakes, entrants agree to be bound by these rules and the decisions of the judges and sweepstakes sponsors, which are final in all matters relating to the sweepstakes.

9. For a list of major prizewinners (available after 7/15/98), send a stamped, self-addressed envelope to Prizewinners, Pocket Books/Sabrina, The Teenage Witch Sweepstakes, 13th Floor, 1230 Avenue of the Americas, NY, NY 10020.

10. Simon & Schuster is the official sweepstakes sponsor.

11. The sweepstakes sponsors shall have no liability for any injury, loss, or damage of any kind arising out of participation in this sweepstakes or the acceptance or use of the prize. Viacom Productions, Paramount Pictures, and Archie Comic Publications, Inc., and their respective parent and affiliated companies are not responsible for fulfillment of prizes or for any loss, damage, or injury suffered as a result of the set tour or use of acceptance of prizes.

Official Entry Form

Name_____

Address_____

City_____ State_____ Zip_____

Phone_____

flexible personnel management in the public service

ORGANISATION FOR ECONOMIC CO-OPERATION AND DEVELOPMENT

O.E.C.D , Paris , 1990

Pursuant to article 1 of the Convention signed in Paris on 14th December 1960, and which came into force on 30th September 1961, the Organisation for Economic Co-operation and Development (OECD) shall promote policies designed:

- to achieve the highest sustainable economic growth and employment and a rising standard of living in Member countries, while maintaining financial stability, and thus to contribute to the development of the world economy;
- to contribute to sound economic expansion in Member as well as non-member countries in the process of economic development; and
- to contribute to the expansion of world trade on a multilateral, non-discriminatory basis in accordance with international obligations.

The original Member countries of the OECD are Austria, Belgium, Canada, Denmark, France, the Federal Republic of Germany, Greece, Iceland, Ireland, Italy, Luxembourg, the Netherlands, Norway, Portugal, Spain, Sweden, Switzerland, Turkey, the United Kingdom and the United States. The following countries became Members subsequently through accession at the dates indicated hereafter: Japan (28th April 1964), Finland (28th January 1969), Australia (7th June 1971) and New Zealand (29th May 1973).

The Socialist Federal Republic of Yugoslavia takes part in some of the work of the OECD (agreement of 28th October 1961).

Publié en français sous le titre:

FLEXIBILITÉ DANS LA GESTION DU PERSONNEL
DE L'ADMINISTRATION PUBLIQUE